Katy Perry
Famous Pop Singer & Songwriter

by Lucas Diver

abdopublishing.com

Published by Abdo Kids, a division of ABDO, PO Box 398166, Minneapolis, Minnesota 55439.

Copyright © 2015 by Abdo Consulting Group, Inc. International copyrights reserved in all countries. No part of this book may be reproduced in any form without written permission from the publisher.

Printed in the United States of America, North Mankato, Minnesota.

102014

012015

THIS BOOK CONTAINS RECYCLED MATERIALS

Photo Credits: AP Images, Corbis, Getty Images, iStock, Landov Media, Shutterstock © Harmony Gerber p.17, © Featureflash p.21 / shutterstock.com

Production Contributors: Teddy Borth, Jennie Forsberg, Grace Hansen

Design Contributors: Laura Rask, Dorothy Toth

Library of Congress Control Number: 2014943782

Cataloging-in-Publication Data

Diver, Lucas.

 Katy Perry: famous pop singer & songwriter / Lucas Diver.

   p. cm. -- (Pop bios)

Includes index.

ISBN 978-1-62970-725-9

1. Perry, Katy--Juvenile literature. 2. Singers--United States--Biography--Juvenile literature. 1. Title.

782.42164092--dc23

[B]

2014943782

Table of Contents

Early Life 4

A Singer From the Start 6

From Katy Hudson
to Katy Perry 12

Hit Maker. 20

Timeline. 22

Glossary 23

Index 24

Abdo Kids Code. 24

Early Life

Katheryn Hudson was born on October 25, 1984. She was born in Santa Barbara, California.

A Singer From the Start

Katy loved to sing. She took lessons. Her parents were **ministers**. She mainly sang **gospel music**.

At age 16, Katy went to Nashville, Tennessee. There, she met people in the music business.

In 2001, Katy recorded a Christian pop album. It did not sell very well. She was known as Katy Hudson then.

From Katy Hudson to Katy Perry

In 2008, Katy signed with a new **label**. She changed her name to Katy Perry. She released a pop album.

Katy's first pop album was a hit! She was chosen for a **Grammy** award. She went on her first **headline** tour.

In 2010, Katy released her second pop album. It featured the song "California Gurls."

In 2013, Katy's third pop album was released. Her hit song "Roar" topped the charts.

Hit Maker

Katy writes most of her music. Her hard work is paying off. She continues to release hit after hit.

Timeline

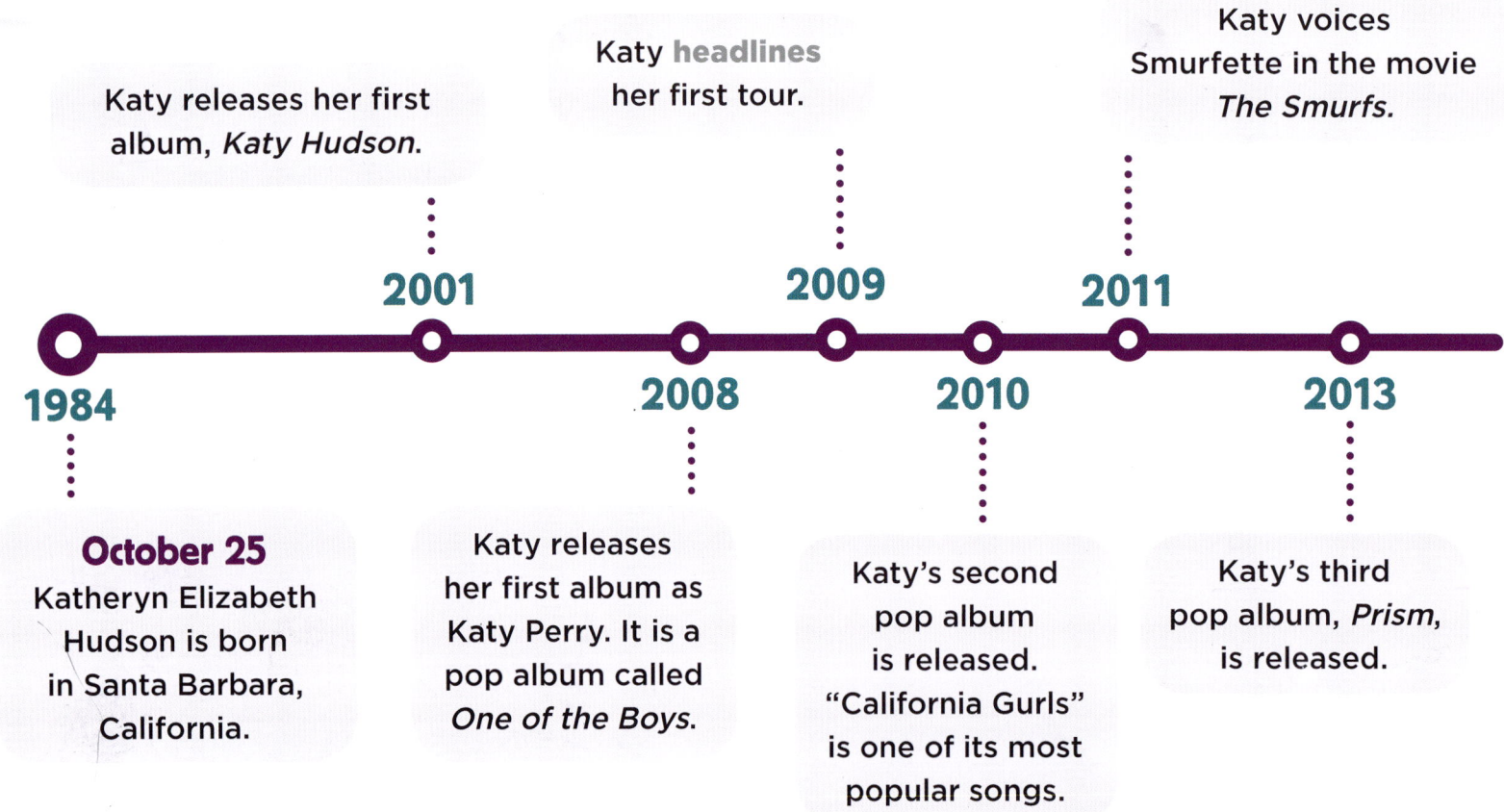

2001 — Katy releases her first album, *Katy Hudson*.

2009 — Katy headlines her first tour.

2011 — Katy voices Smurfette in the movie *The Smurfs*.

1984 — **October 25** Katheryn Elizabeth Hudson is born in Santa Barbara, California.

2008 — Katy releases her first album as Katy Perry. It is a pop album called *One of the Boys*.

2010 — Katy's second pop album is released. "California Gurls" is one of its most popular songs.

2013 — Katy's third pop album, *Prism*, is released.

Glossary

gospel music – a music genre in Christian music.

Grammy – a small statue that is given as an award to someone who works in the music business.

headline – the main act of a concert tour.

label – short for record label. A record label is a company that produces, creates, distributes, and markets an artist's album, and more.

minister – a person whose job it is to lead church services, perform religious ceremonies, and more.

Index

album 10, 12, 14, 16, 18

birth 4

"California Gurls" 16

Capital Records 12

family 6

Grammy 14

Nashville, Tennessee 8

"Roar" 18

Santa Barbara, California 4

tour 14

abdokids.com

Use this code to log on to abdokids.com and access crafts, games, videos, and more!

Abdo Kids Code:
PKK7259

Tempe PT
4/17

ML

10-15